THER

Jane Chapman

LITTLE TIGER

LONDON

Hidden under shady leaves,
a tiny face peeps out.
Silent. Alone.

Outside,
the world
is strange
and shadowy.

But rain clouds bring
sweet water,

wind brings the
smell of food . . .

and something else.
Something new,
something BIG.
Something . . .

. . . . scary.

But behind this
fearsome face is kindness.
A soft hand.

A friend who will

share their feast . . .

Who will bring
a smile . . .

And make the world

feel safe again . . .

Even magical.

Some days the world may still seem full of shadows.

But that friend
will be there
to share
adventures . . .

and find
happiness . . .

Together.